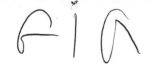

Alec and His Flying Bed

SIMON BUCKINGHAM

Lothrop, Lee & Shepard Books
New York

Copyright © 1990 by Simon Buckingham

First published in Great Britain by
Macmillan Children's Books

Printed in Hong Kong

First U.S. edition 1991

1 2 3 4 5 6 7 8 9 10

Library of Congress Cataloguing in Publication
data was not available in time for publication
of this book, but can now be obtained from
either the publisher or the Library of Congress

ISBN 0-688-10555-6

ISBN 0-688-10556-4 (lib.)

LC Number: 90-52939

Alec passed the rubbish dump every afternoon on his way home from school.
He noticed the old bed at once, perched on top of a pile of rubbish.

He put down his bike and scrambled up to take a closer look. It was made of
iron and had wheels like a hospital bed.

Carefully, he pulled the bed down from the heap. It moved quite easily over the rough ground. He really liked it; it was much better than the one he had at home. I wonder if Mum will let me keep it, he thought. Then he decided—he *would* take it home. So he put his bike on top and trundled off.

When he got home a neighbor called out, "Moving house, are you, lad?"

Alec ignored him. He hoped he could get the bed up to his room without his mother noticing, but she was watching out for him.

"What on earth are you doing with that dreadful old thing?" she called. "I hope you're not going to bring it in here. I don't want it in my house. Besides, it won't even go through the door."

"Oh, please, Mum," said Alec. "It comes apart. Please?"

"Oh, all right, then," his mother said, "but just you be careful." And she went off to get his supper ready.

But it was not all right. Alec was struggling up the stairs with the last piece when he knocked a picture off the wall. The glass shattered with a loud crash.

His mother rushed out of the kitchen.

"You careless boy!" she cried. "Clean up that mess and go to your room. If you like that old bed so much you can lie on it and stay there till morning."

Alec was fed up, stuck in his room with no supper, no TV, and a long, boring evening ahead. He was just going to get a book from the shelf when something very odd happened.

He felt the bed move! It had definitely moved! Am I dreaming? he wondered. Then he felt a jolt and the bed slowly tilted to one side. He looked down. To his amazement, the bed was hovering above the floor. Alec sat tight. It was too late to get off now. Slowly, silently, the bed was moving toward the open window.

He was flying! He was really flying!

He found he could make the bed climb higher by sitting at one end. He
moved to the other end and it started to go down. He tried moving to the edge. . . .
Suddenly the bed went into a banking turn. Alec clung tightly.

Easy does it, no sudden movements, he thought as he leveled out again.
Soon he was flying over the countryside, high up in the fresh evening air.
Alec was really enjoying himself now.

He decided to land in the field below. This is easy, he thought as he made a quick turn to avoid a tree. But he was going too fast and suddenly, right ahead, he saw a man fishing.

Before Alec knew what was happening, the man had fallen into the water.
"Help! Help! I can't swim!" Alec heard the man shout.
He had control of the bed again and, hovering over the water, he managed to help the man clamber aboard.

"Crikey!" said the man. "What's going on? What's happening?" He leaned over the edge of the bed. "Blimey! What is this thing? We're right up in the air!"

"I'm sorry, mister," said Alec. "I lost control."

"Look, son, I don't know who you are or what this flying contraption is, but I need to get back to the circus at Middleton. I work there—I'm Bozo."

"Okay," said Alec. He knew where Middleton was. He could fly there.

Just as they were getting near the circus, a gaggle of geese came flying by.

"Hold still, lad," whispered Bozo, "here comes our dinner."

"Be careful!" cried Alec. "You'll capsize us!"

The bed tipped sideways. Alec lost his balance and fell. . . .

Down and down he went, the wind roaring in his ears. Alec shut his eyes tight.

He was heading straight for the circus tent!
He burst through the canvas roof—falling, falling.

He heard a great gasp from the audience.

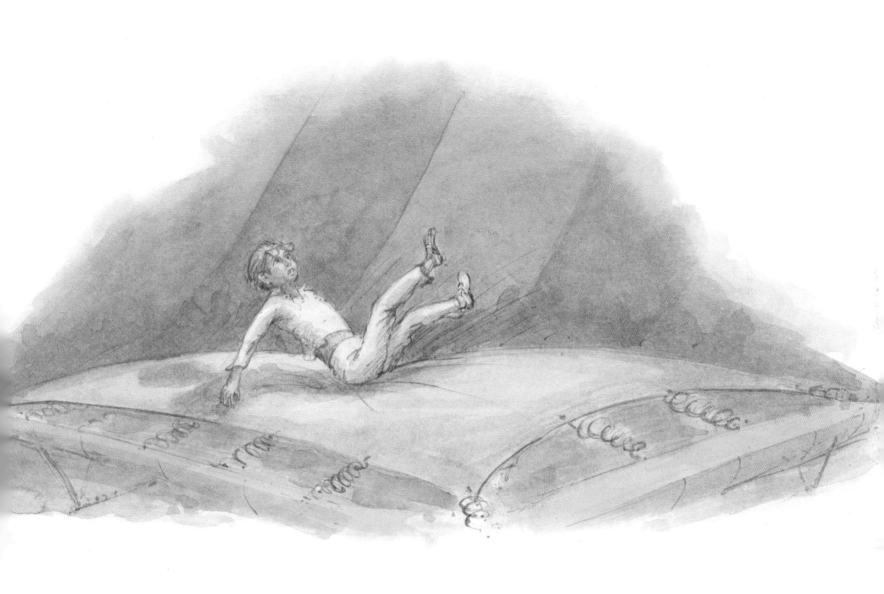

Then he felt something give way beneath him and throw him back into the air.

Up he soared.
"Grab hold of my wrists!" he heard a voice call.

He clung to the man's wrists—but how long could he hold on?

The audience was wild with excitement. It was the most amazing circus act anyone had ever seen.

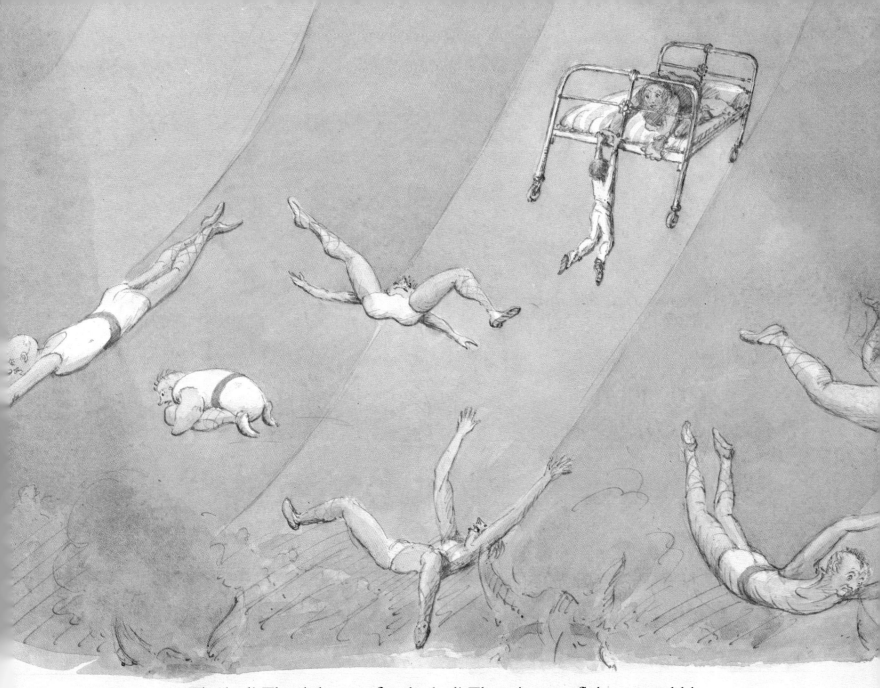

The bed! Thank heaven for the bed! There it was—flying toward him.
Bozo caught Alec's hands and managed to haul him aboard.

"Phew! That was a close shave," said Bozo.
"I thought I'd lost you back there."

Alec, breathless and not sure whether he was on
his head or his heels, couldn't say a word.

They landed outside the tent, close to a small trailer.

"Cheer up, lad, I think we both deserve a good supper after all that. Let's see what's cooking at home."

It was the best supper that Alec had ever tasted—chips, beans, bacon, eggs, and sausage. He felt full and rather sleepy. I really ought to be getting home now, he thought. . . .

It was very odd. He could still smell bacon frying, but it was a bright sunny morning and he was back in his own room!

There was his mother standing in the doorway.

"I'm sorry I was cross with you yesterday," she said. "Come on, sleepyhead, your breakfast's ready."

Alec yawned and shook his head.

"Mum," he said, "I've just had the weirdest dream. . . ."